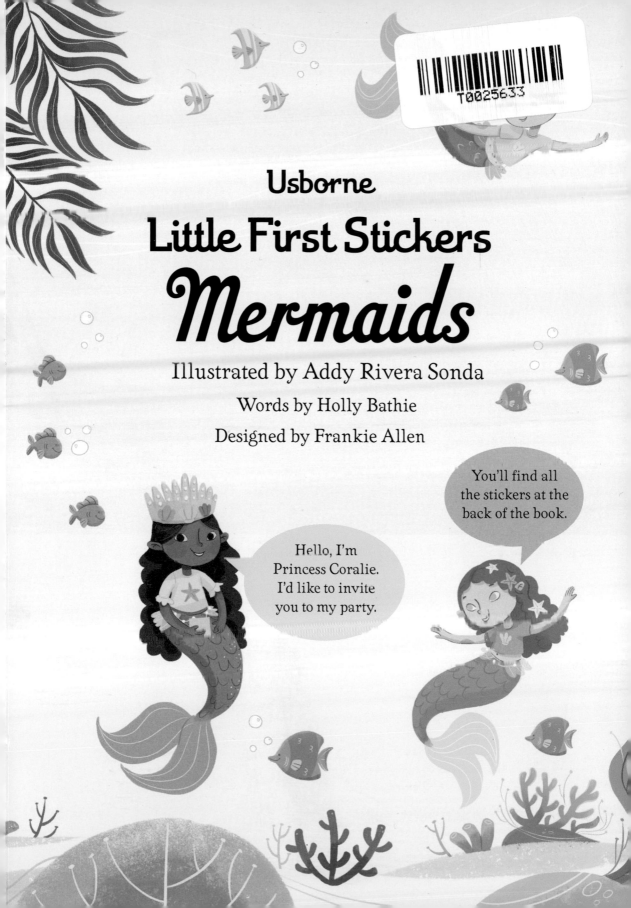

Usborne

# Little First Stickers
# Mermaids

Illustrated by Addy Rivera Sonda

Words by Holly Bathie

Designed by Frankie Allen

You'll find all the stickers at the back of the book.

Hello, I'm Princess Coralie. I'd like to invite you to my party.

# In the lagoon

The lagoon is full of lovely shells for these mermaids to add to their outfits for Princess Coralie's birthday party.

Stick on some more shells for the mermaids to find.

Add more mermaids, with the shells they have collected.

# Shipwreck

A hiding mermaid has spotted some shiny jewels for Princess Coralie. Add more diving mermaids, and treasure for them to find.

Stick on some angelfish.

# Getting ready

Choose pretty accessories to help these mermaids get ready for Coralie's party.

Give the mermaids pretty party tails and necklaces.

Put stars and
shells in the
mermaids' hair.

Stick on the
mermaids'
shell bags.

# The guests arrive

Coralie's guests are arriving at the palace. Stick on all the seahorses and their riders.

Add more fish to the scene.

# Inside the palace

Stick Princess Coralie on her throne, then add all of her friends bringing her presents.

Add more party guests with their drinks.

# In the ballroom

The mermaids love to dance.
Stick on the birthday mermaid
and her friends dancing to the music.

Stick another crab
musician here.

# Mermaid bedtime

After a wonderful party, the mermaids are tired from all that dancing! Put all the sleepy mermaids in their shell and coral beds.

Add some jellyfish nightlights to the scene.

14

Find a place for a mermaid reading a bedtime story.

15

# Presents

Help Princess Coralie open her gifts.
Stick all her lovely presents on this page.